# Otto
# Learns About His Medicine

Published by
**M A G I N A T I O N   P R E S S**
An Educational Publishing Foundation Book
American Psychological Association
750 First Street, NE
Washington, DC 20002

For more information about our books, including a complete catalog, please write to us, call 1-800-374-2721, or visit our website at www.maginationpress.com.

Editor: Darcie Conner Johnston
Art Director: Susan K. White
The text type is Bookman

Library of Congress Cataloging-in-Publication Data

Galvin, Matthew.
Otto learns about his medicine : a story about medication for children with ADHD / by Matthew Galvin ; illustrated by Sandra Ferraro.—3rd ed.
p.  cm.
Summary: Otto, a fidgety young car that has trouble paying attention in school, visits a special mechanic who prescribes a medicine to control his hyperactive behavior.
ISBN 1-55798-771-8 (hc. : alk. paper)—ISBN 1-55798-772-6 (pbk. : alk paper)
[1. Hyperactive children—Fiction. 2. Attention-deficit hyperactivity disorder—Fiction. 3. Automobiles—Fiction.] I. Ferraro, Sandra, ill. II. Title.
PZ7.G1423 Ot 2001                                                          2001030621
[E]—dc21

Manufactured in the United States of America
10 9 8 7 6 5 4 3 2 1

# Otto
# Learns About His Medicine

## A Story About Medication For Children With ADHD

THIRD EDITION

written by Matthew Galvin M.D.
illustrated by Sandra Ferraro

MAGINATION PRESS • WASHINGTON, DC

nce upon a time, far away, there was a land where cars grew up much as people do. They talked as people do, and they lived in families as people do.

Otto liked being a car. He knew he had a lot to learn because he was still very young. He had to learn about traffic lights, road signs, and how to drive on wet, slippery pavement.

So Otto went to school five days a week. When young cars go to school, they study in the classroom. They also go out on a track where they practice following directions and controlling their speed.

7

Otto wanted to learn, but he had some problems. First of all, he could not pay attention in class. He tried to listen to his teacher, Mr. Jalopey, but before he knew it, he stopped listening. He looked out the window, or watched his classmates, or listened to cars passing by. Then, when he tried to listen to Mr. Jalopey again, he had missed so much of the class that he was lost.

When Mr. Jalopey said, "Everyone pay attention,"
Otto tried. But Otto could not pay attention to just one
thing—no matter how important it was—for very long.
So Otto did not learn how to tell how much gasoline was
in his tank, or how fast he was going, or how to figure
out how many miles he had gone on a trip.

Otto also had a terrible time getting his homework done. One day the class was asked to draw a line on a road map to show how to get from one city to another. Now, Otto knew just how to go, because he had been on the very same trip with his parents. But he could not use the road map.

He couldn't keep one place on the map in his mind long enough while he searched for the next place to go. He brought his homework to school and honked and honked and honked until Mr. Jalopey asked him what the matter was. Otto said, "I need help with my homework." Mr. Jalopey helped him. Otto honked again and said, "I need help again." Finally Mr. Jalopey told Otto he was calling out in class too much.

Then there was the problem of how to stop and think. One day Otto was learning how to fill up his gas tank. He was almost finished at the pump when he noticed his friend Rod's new racing stripes. Without thinking, he drove off after Rod. The hose yanked out of Otto's tank when he sped away. It sprayed gasoline on everyone, even Mr. Jalopey.

As if all that weren't
enough, there was yet
another thing. Otto could
not keep still. When
everyone
lined up on
the track,
Otto would rev up his
motor. Then Otto went back and forth,
gearing up to take off. Sometimes he
bumped into the car in front of him.
Sometimes he bumped into the car
behind him. The other cars got mad
and honked their horns. Sometimes
they even bumped Otto right back.

Finally Mr. Jalopey called Otto's mom and dad in for a talk. Otto's mom, Mrs. Mobile, sighed and said she had hoped Otto would settle down once he was in school. "He has always been on the go," Mr. Mobile added.

They decided that Otto would go to see a special mechanic who knew how to talk to young cars. Her name was Dr. Wheeler.

Before Otto went to visit Dr. Wheeler, his parents and his teacher filled out some forms and checklists answering questions about what Otto was like.

On the day of the visit, Otto and Dr. Wheeler talked awhile. Otto said, "My motor always goes too fast. I can't help it." Dr. Wheeler told Otto that sometimes young cars have that kind of trouble. She asked him lots of questions about school, and home, and even his friendships with the other cars. Afterward, she said, "Your motor does go too fast, Otto. And that makes it harder for you to control yourself. It makes it harder for you to listen in school and to keep still when you want to. It makes you want to move all the time."

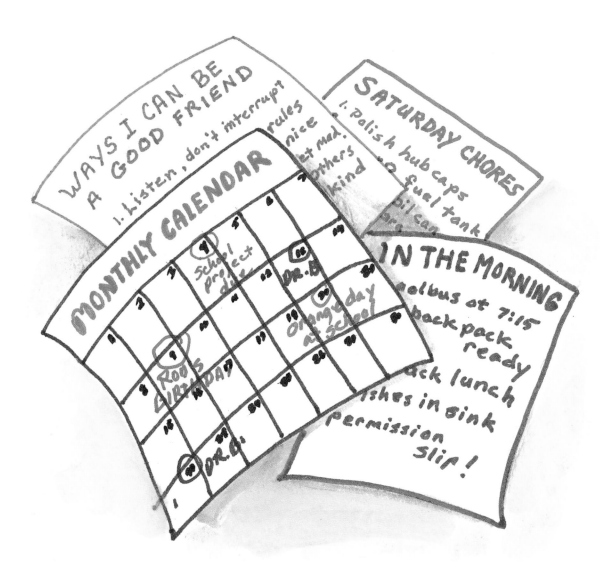

Otto wanted to know what he could do about his fast motor. Otto's parents wanted to know, too. Dr. Wheeler said that she would help Otto learn how to decide what is most important to pay attention to in school. She would show him lots of ways to remember things, keep track of his homework, and even how to get along better with the other cars. She would work with Mr. Jalopey in school. And she would show Mr. and Mrs. Mobile how they could help Otto at home.

"Think of us as your pit crew, Otto," she said with a smile. "Not to help you go as fast as you possibly can but instead to help you go the best that you can." Otto liked the idea of having his own pit crew that included his parents, his teacher, and Dr. Wheeler. But that was not all.

Dr. Wheeler said that besides Otto's parents, Mr. Jalopey, and herself, there was someone else she thought should be a member of Otto's pit crew. She said Otto probably needed a special car medicine. To learn about this medicine, Otto would need to see someone else who worked with Dr. Wheeler, a different special mechanic whose name was Dr. Beemer.

Otto and his parents went to see Dr. Beemer.
Just like Dr. Wheeler, Dr. Beemer asked Otto lots
of questions. Some questions were the same as
Dr. Wheeler's, and some were different. He asked
about times when Otto was sick and when he was
well. He asked what kind of gas was Otto's favorite.

He also asked if he could look under Otto's hood.
He checked the oil. He checked the headlights. He
checked everything. Dr. Beemer said, "Otto, I think
Dr. Wheeler is right. There is a medicine that may
help you." This medicine would help Otto keep still
long enough and pay attention long enough to
learn what he needed to know.

Otto wondered if the medicine would make him do things like sit still and follow all the rules. Dr. Beemer said, "No, Otto, medicine will not make you do any of those things. All that this medicine can do is *let* you be a better listener and help you choose to pay attention and choose to stay still." Otto still had to learn how to listen, what to pay attention to, and when it was better to go fast or to go slow. These were the kinds of things that his pit crew would teach him.

RRRRUMBLE

Otto was also worried about the
medicine because his friend Rod was
sick once with a sore muffler. The
medicine Rod had to take really
helped his sore muffler, but it also
made him rumble. So Otto knew
that the medicine could help, but it
could also do funny things.

Otto's mechanic explained that most medicines can have some side effects. Side effects are the things that might happen that nobody especially likes about medicine. A lot of times they do not happen at all or they are not too bad. The most common side effects of this medicine were that it might make Otto less hungry and less sleepy.

Dr. Beemer told Otto and his parents that he had given the special medicine to many young cars. The medicine had been available for a long time, and mechanics had learned a lot about it. Dr. Beemer had some ideas about how to make the side effects better if they happened at all. Otto would take the medicine only at certain times of the day so that it would not keep him awake and would not make him less hungry.

He promised that Otto would have check-ups. At the check-ups, Dr. Beemer would measure Otto's height and weight and ask if he had any side effects. He said Otto would get check-ups as often as he needed to while Otto worked with Dr. Wheeler. As members of Otto's pit crew, Dr. Beemer and Dr. Wheeler would talk together. Dr. Wheeler would ask Otto's parents and teacher what Otto was like on and off his medicine, and she would share this information with the pit crew. This way they could find out if the medicine was working. He could also tell if the medicine was still needed to help Otto do the job that needed doing.

It was almost time to go. Otto had learned that he was not alone, that other young cars had problems like his. He had learned that there were things he could do that would help him slow down and pay attention. And he had learned that there were special medicines that could help too. Otto had a lot to think about. Most of all, he was glad that he had his mom and dad and all the special mechanics in his pit crew to help him learn how to be the best car he could be.

# Note to Parents for the Third Edition

*Otto Learns About His Medicine* was written for young persons with Attention Deficit Hyperactivity Disorder (ADHD). Specifically, it was written for hyperactive children who have been prescribed medications for ADHD. However, it may also be of interest to their siblings and peers, helping them understand the behavior and appreciate the problems faced by the child whose "motor goes too fast."

Using the easily grasped metaphor of a car whose engine runs too fast, this story describes some of the effects of ADHD: trouble paying attention, trouble focusing on just one thing, trouble keeping still, trouble thinking before acting, trouble learning in school. It lets children know that they are not alone in having these problems. And it shows some of the kinds of help available from health care and mental health care professionals, with a special focus on medication. A comprehensive treatment also includes cognitive and behavioral counseling for the child, parental training that is sensitive to special needs of the child with ADHD, and school interventions (e.g., daily report cards or notebooks that travel among members of the treatment team). In this book, the members of the treatment team are called the "pit crew."

Children may be worried or frightened regarding medication. This book can help, in that information can reduce their worries and correct unrealistic ideas. Many different medications are available for use in ADHD. Often the first choice is from the family of medications called psychostimulants. The term "stimulant" sometimes creates confusion. I am often asked, "Won't a *stimulant* cause my child to be even more hyperactive? I definitely don't want that!" Neither does your doctor. It is helpful to think of these medications as stimulating the pathways in the brain that allow a person to focus and to make more efficient use of their working memory and problem-solving skills. Problem-solving skills include:

1. Stopping and recognizing there's a problem to be solved;
2. Thinking through alternative ways of solving it;
3. Thinking about the consequences of each alternative solution;
4. Choosing a solution based on how those consequences are valued;
5. Devising a strategy for implementing the solution.

In daily living, things happen and people respond. In shorthand, let's say S (denoting *something happens*) is followed by R (denoting a person's *response*), or S-R. Think of the hyphen between S and R as a way to represent the chance to focus. In a person with ADHD, the hyphen is shorter than it is in others. Medications draw the hyphen out more, from S-R to, say, S—-R. It is important to understand that medication doesn't fill in the hyphen, though. Medication doesn't think things through or make one mindful of alternatives, consequences, values, or strategies.

The person has to do all that, although the "pit crew" can help the person acquire problem-solving and other necessary skills.

Stimulants include preparations of methylphenidate and dextroamphetamine. Newer forms of both of these medications offer advantages over older forms with respect to duration and side effects. Side effects of stimulants can be classified as common, infrequent, or rare. Appetite suppression and insomnia are fairly common side effects that can typically be managed by timing and dosage of medication. Another possible side effect is a slowing down in the rate of a child's growth. This occurs infrequently, and in the vast majority of cases the stimulant-induced changes in growth velocity do not affect the height attained by adulthood. However, any slowing down of growth may be a concern for the child who is at a very low percentile of height or weight for his or her age.

Involuntary movements known as "tics" (e.g., eye-blinking or facial twitches) are a rare side effect. Tics are often attributed to a condition called Tourette's syndrome, in which all or some of the symptoms of ADHD emerge first and are treated with stimulants. The tics arise only later in the natural course of Tourette's and are sometimes erroneously attributed to the medication. Nonetheless, in some cases there may be an aggravation of tics by stimulants that is sufficient to warrant discontinuation of the stimulant or addition of a tic-suppressing medication.

The choice of medication may be quite different if there are accompanying conditions or disorders. Antidepressants may be prescribed for children who have depression or anxiety in addition to their ADHD. Also in use, as stated above, are medications that act as tic suppressants; these are neither stimulants nor antidepressants. Sometimes more than one medication is required. It is important to note that some of the choices are *off-label*, so called because they have not been approved for treating ADHD or children below certain ages by the Food and Drug Administration, but there is some base of evidence for their use.

Parents often inquire about alternative medicine, including herbal remedies and nutritional supplements. I do not doubt that some will turn out to have value. However, they should be viewed according to the same rigorous requirements of evidence as any other treatment or medication. More important to keep in mind is that medication is just part of the treatment plan, and the prescribing authority is just one member of the pit crew.

This story will help children and their parents have realistic expectations about what medications for ADHD can and can't do. It is not intended to replace ongoing discussions about ADHD or its treatment with the physician, other prescribing authority, or any other member of the interdisciplinary treatment team. Rather, it is hoped that the story will help children and their parents bring greater awareness and comfort to these ongoing discussions within the family and with professionals.

MATTHEW GALVIN, M.D.

# About the Author

Matthew Galvin, M.D., is a psychiatrist with an expertise in children and adolescents, as well as the author of several books on topics of special concern to young people. He also teaches, writes, and conducts research in the areas of conscience formation and professional ethics. Dr. Galvin lives with his family in Indiana.

# About the Illustrator

Sandra Laramore Ferraro is both a special education teacher for children and an artist who concentrates mainly in oil painting and printmaking. She has collaborated with Matthew Galvin on several children's books, contributing her highly colorful and energetic illustrations. She lives in Indiana with her son and two daughters.

# More Books About ADD and ADHD From Magination Press

**The Best of "BRAKES": An Activity Book for Kids with ADD**
Edited by Patricia Quinn, M.D., and Judith Stern, M.A.
*From the pages of the BRAKES newsletter for kids with ADD, this collection features all the best articles, games, puzzles, helpful hints, and resources. Ages 8-13.*

**Help Is on the Way: A Child's Book About ADD**
By Marc Nemiroff, Ph.D., and Jane Annunziata, Psy.D., illustrated by Margaret Scott.
*With upbeat language and vibrant illustrations, this book describes how children experience the symptoms of ADD, how they can cope with it, and what kind of help is available. Ages 5-9.*

**Learning to Slow Down and Pay Attention (2nd Edition)**
By Kathleen Nadeau, Ph.D., and Ellen Dixon, Ph.D., illustrated by John Rose.
*This fun, friendly workbook offers a wealth of helpful tips for every situation—at home, at school, and among friends and family. Ages 6-10.*

**Sparky's Excellent Misadventures: My A.D.D. Journal, by Me (Sparky)**
By Phyllis Carpenter and Marti Ford, illustrated by Peter Horjus.
*This fictional week-in-the-life account of a smart, funny, lovable kid with ADD is full of information, self-help tips, optimism, empowerment, and fun. Ages 5-11.*

*To order, visit our website at www.maginationpress.com or call 1-800-374-2721.*